NICK JR. WONDER PETS!

Good Night, Wonder Pets!

by Josh Selig
illustrated by Little Airplane Productions

SIMON SPOTLIGHT/ NICK JR.

New York   London   Toronto   Sydney

"Come on, Wonder Pets!" Linny said.
"Let's put the baby animals to bed!"

They helped a frog into a puddle
for his bath and a little cuddle.

They brushed the teeth of a crocodile.
She went to sleep with a gleaming smile!

They flew out West with a cozy pillow
and tucked in a baby armadillo.

They sang a song of sweet *moo-moo*s,
and soon the cow began to snooze.

They helped a penguin who was chilly.
He warmed up, but he looked silly.

They gave a little bee a hug,
and soon she was a sleepy bug.

They said good night to a baby skunk,
but held their noses 'cause he stunk.

Then the Wonder Pets flew home fast
because their bedtime had come at last.

They had some celery, turned off the light,
and said, "Good night,
good night,
good night!"